DILLY
FOR
PRESIDENT

By Cynthia L. Copeland

Millbrook Press
Minneapolis

For Alex, my little Dilly

Acknowlegements:
Thanks to Amy Shields for starting it all, and to Alex and Anja
for letting me use their fabulous ideas.

And thank you to my friends at Fuller Elementary School,
especially Mrs. Toscano.

Millbrook Press
A division of Lerner Publishing Group
241 First Avenue North
Minneapolis, MN 55401 U.S.A.

Website address: www.lernerbooks.com

Library of Congress Cataloging-in-Publication Data

Copeland, Cynthia L.
    Dilly for President / Cynthia L. Copeland.
        p. cm.
    Summary: In her journal, Dilly describes her campaign for president of the fourth-grade class, and how she learns to deal with the responsibilities when she wins the election.
        ISBN-13: 978−0−7613−2372−3 (lib. bdg.)
        ISBN-10: 0−7613−2372−4 (lib. bdg.)
        [1. Elections—Fiction. 2. Schools—Fiction. 3. Diaries—Fiction.] I. Title.
    PZ7.C78797Di 2006
    [Fic−dc22]   2003017946

Manufactured in the United States of America
1 2 3 4 5 6 − JR − 11 10 09 08 07 06

Dear _Dilly_,

Welcome to fourth grade! As part of our Reading unit this first marking period, you will be keeping a journal.

-You must write in your journal at least three times a week.
-You must use good fourth grade sentences.
-You may illustrate your journal.
-You may write about anything.

Please begin your journal with a page or two about yourself. Describe your family and some of your likes and dislikes.

This is YOUR journal. You will not be asked to share anything that you write with the class. I will grade it at the end of the marking period.

Mrs. T

September 4

Well, I can think of a MUCH more interesting way to begin a journal than to write about ME, but I don't want to start off fourth grade with a big, fat "F."

So here goes . . .

Name: Dilly Duncan
("Dilly" is my nickname, but I will NEVER EVER tell my real name unless I am tortured with cheese.)

Parents:
Two: one of each

Brother:
One: Matthew
Status: Annoying

Stuff I hate:

1. **CHEESE!**

2. When people spit on the ground and you can see it

3. When hot toast makes the peanut butter drippy

Stuff I like:

1. Frogs

2. Long, shiny black hair

3. Bacon sandwiches

Favorite bird: Blue-footed booby

Favorite way to draw stars:

Favorite TV show:

Lassie reruns.

My dad used to watch it when he was little!

Favorite letter
to write in cursive:

I wish my name was

Lilly Luncan

Second favorite letter
to write in cursive:

Favorite number:

cute, shy little

FANCY
ones

Things I want:

Glasses

A motorcycle

A boa constrictor

Things I don't want:

Pimples

Buck teeth

What I looked like when I was a baby:

← drool
(ew!)

What I look like now:

me in the sloppy growing-out stage

← I want to grow my bangs out but my mom says the growing-out stage is sloppy looking

← necklace I found outside the YMCA

What I will look like when I am 100:

← drool
(ew!)

Best friend since kindergarten:

She hates her freckles and her chin dimple. I like her freckles but the chin dimple is a little funky.

Meredith

Meredith trivia question: What is the name of her gerbil?

Answer: Mr. Chicken

7

September 5

It's kind of fun coming back to school after summer vacation. I like seeing all of my friends again and hearing about the cool stuff they did. (Cammy went white-water rafting! Lucky!)

At recess today, the girls claimed the big climbing spider. We have to do that at the start of every year so the new boys know that it's for **GIRLS ONLY.** The boys hang out under the twirly slide but most of the time they're running around.

GIRLS RULE!

I can't believe how much some kids changed over the summer!

Kate (who borrowed my snake ring in second grade and **NEVER GAVE IT BACK!**) has little boobies now and her hair got blonder.

Dillon Cobb has always had little boobies and now he also has glasses that pinch his nose. He thinks that wearing glasses makes him smarter. (He can use all the help he can get.)

Annie got braces and has to wear her headgear to school sometimes. Pooooor Annie. . . .

Blaine got taller AND goofier, if that's possible. I think his bobo ears are even more bobo.

Cammy got 7½ inches cut off her hair! She wears it behind her ears to show off her extra hole. She wears a little bunny stud in it—**LUCKY!**

Lauren is the funniest girl in the whole world and over the summer she just got funnier. In August she got 7 new fish for her tank. She named them Sunday, Monday, Tuesday, Wednesday, Thursday, Friday, and Chuck.

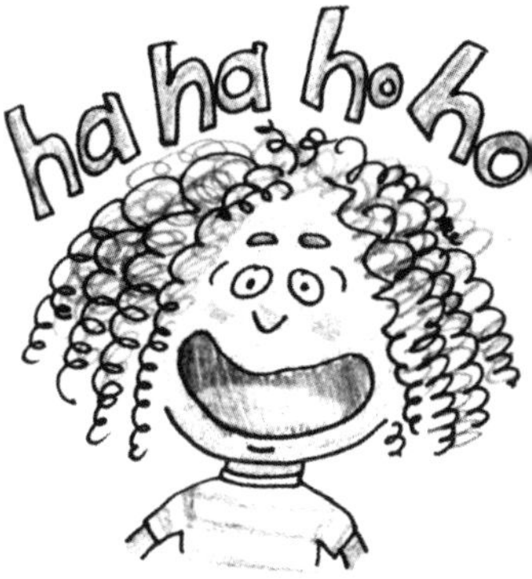
ha ha ho ho

The other kids haven't changed all that much. Griffin and Sam show off for the girls all the time and Beanie just has lots more freckles like she does at the end of every summer. Stuart still sucks his thumb when he thinks no one is looking. Meredith didn't change one single bit and neither did I.

Two kids in my class are **NEW**, so I have no idea whether or not they changed. It's time for Math now so I'll write about them on Monday.

September 8

Meredith and I decided to be twins today. We are wearing matching shirts and "Princess" socks. You can hardly tell us apart!

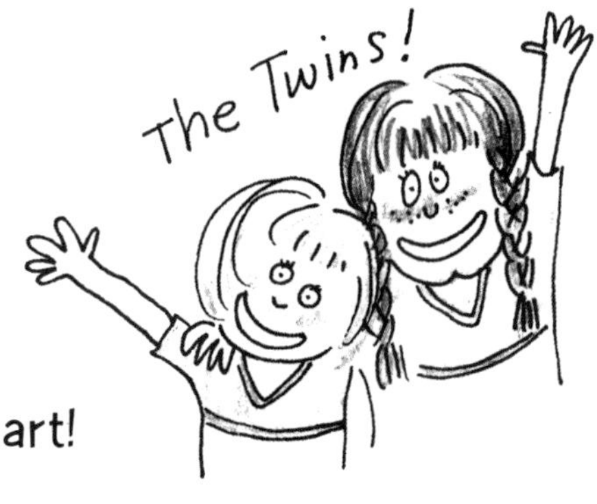
The Twins!

I promised on Friday that I would tell about the new kids.

Rachel Something-or-other (who sits right in front of me) wears this glitter stuff in her hair and on her cheeks. Sometimes, when the sun comes in through the window just right, she's so shiny I have to squint my eyes to see the board.

Titus Stout is from Wisconsin. He just moved here last week. He said Wisconsin is famous for cheese. **THANK GOODNESS I DON'T LIVE THERE!!** It's funny that his name is "stout" because that means fat and he's so skinny. He's kind of quiet. He doesn't laugh at Sam's dopey jokes like the other boys do. He has a backpack EXACTLY like mine and his hook is right next to mine so it's going to make things VERY confusing.

Meredith and I had to be the guards of the climbing spider today while the girls were meeting because Blaine kept on trying to get close enough to hear what we were talking about.

We were talking about how Mrs. Hamlin, who teaches second grade, says planet "erf" instead of planet "earth" but we pretended we were telling secrets about boys. **Hee hee!**

Mrs. Hamlin has taught here for at least 100 years and she looks exactly the same as when she started. She even has the same glasses. I know that because there is a picture in the office from a REALLY long time ago when the school didn't even have an auditorium and she looks exactly the same.

With her class pet, a dinosaur, a long, long time ago

With her class pet, an iguana, today

There are also pictures in the office of Mr. Cunningham, Mrs. Barry, and Mrs. White, who never change either.

PRINCIPAL

Come in children... WAHAHA HAAAA AAA

Mr. Cunningham, the principal, is very nice but everyone is afraid to be sent to his office. I wonder what is in there besides him.

Everyone calls the school secretary "Scary Mrs. Barry." Maybe the thing that kids don't like about getting sent to the principal's office is that they have to sit next to Mrs. Barry while they are waiting to see Mr. Cunningham.

Mrs. White is the school nurse. Her office is part of the principal's office and it's like a little Wal-Mart. She has extra socks if yours get wet, ponytail holders, even extra underpants. In kindergarten Meredith wet her pants and she got butterfly underpants to KEEP.

September 10

So far I am definitely liking fourth grade. In third grade, we weren't really the little kids and we weren't really the big kids. Now we're big kids (even though the fifth graders can boss us around if they really want to).

Mrs. Tuckerman, my teacher this year, is very nice. We call her "Mrs. T." So far, she has started off every day by saying, "How can I be so lucky? I get the BEST fourth graders EVERY YEAR!"

She said that she will give us a penny every time she gets our names wrong. So far, Cammy has three pennies 'cause Mrs. T keeps calling her "Kimmy." I don't have any. I must be very memorable.

Mrs. T has a squeaky desk drawer that has Tootsie Rolls in it. Sometimes she gives them to kids who are being really good and sometimes I see her sneak one for herself.

September 11

Mrs. T started a unit on Presidents today. We learned that Thomas Jefferson was the first person in the country to grow a tomato. People in those days thought tomatoes were poisonous! (My mom sprinkles sugar on MY tomatoes so that I will eat them.)

We're also studying the election process and—
HERE'S THE COOL PART—we're going to have our own election for President! There will be one Class President and the other kids will be in Congress. And then we will pass real laws that everyone will have to follow!!! (BUT Mrs. T is the Supreme Court and she could say "no" to the laws if she wanted to.)

It would be fun to be **Class President.**

Being Class President would be good practice for being the REAL President.

Why I want to be the **REAL** President:

1. You could invite ALL your friends for a sleepover in the White House because it has 132 rooms. They could even bring their pets.

2. You could swim in the White House pool or watch movies in the White House theater or bowl in the White House bowling alley. Or you could have one of the White House elevators turned into an ESCALATOR, which is way more fun. And since you're the boss of everyone, you could run UP the DOWN escalator and no one would tell you to quit it!

3. You could change the colors of the flag to aqua, yellow, and orange because everyone is getting pretty tired of red, white, and blue. You could also change the national anthem to something people can actually sing, like "Happy Birthday to You" (but instead of "birthday" we could say "America").

4. You could make laws like: "Every kid gets her own pony to ride around on," and "School doesn't start until I wake up and mosey on over."

5. You would always have those big Secret Service guys all around in case a bully like Anthony Loomis from Mr. Fowler's class tried to beat you up.

6. Your mother would be very proud of you.

September 15

The new girl Rachel is **SO** annoying.

Here's what happened at recess today:
Inside the spider, Rachel showed us this fake tattoo around her belly button. It was supposed to be a wreath of flowers or something stupid like that.

Then she went and told Mrs. T that we were being mean. But I don't think that Mrs. T believed her because we didn't get into trouble or anything. Plus I'll bet she even annoys Mrs. T. Mrs. T probably complains about her to Mr. T when she gets home.

Here's an interesting presidential fact we learned today:

Hiram Ulysses Grant didn't like his initials (**HUG**)
so he changed his name to Ulysses Simpson Grant
before he became President!

Other initials that would be bad to have:

DUM   KIS   YUK
POO   PEE   GAG
            PIG

September 18

Before school started today, everybody was talking about how they want to run for President except Meredith (she doesn't want to run against me) and Dillon Cobb.

The election process is too truculentally artifactual

(No one understands him. It's the glasses talking.)

18

This morning Mrs. T told us how the whole election thing will go. She said that first we will have a primary election where we will vote to pick two candidates. The two kids who get the most votes run against each other in an election in a few weeks. I know I have Meredith's vote and my own vote (unless I say something I really don't agree with, in which case I will vote for someone else).

In Math today, we got to make up our OWN Math problems. Here's mine.

Problem: Susan picked 25 apples. Three were rotten and had brown spots so she threw them at her brother Billy who probably deserved it. Billy shook the tree Susan was standing under and 52 apples fell and all of them except 4 hit Susan on the head and she had to be rushed to the hospital where the doctor gave her 13 stitches.

Question: How many extra chores should Billy have to do for picking on poor Susan?

Answer: 10 (Subtract the 3 apples Susan threw from the number of stitches, 13.)

It was fun. Meredith wrote one about chickens.
Mrs. T is going to type up a worksheet with all of our
word problems on it for us to do next week!

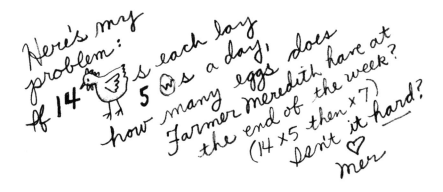

Here's my problem:
If 14 🐔's each lay 5 🥚s a day, how many eggs does Farmer meredith have at the end of the week?
(14 x5 then x7)
Isn't it hard? ♡
mer

Tomorrow we start the Presidential election process!!

September 19

I had to stay in for
morning recess because I
got overly involved in my
cursive and never finished.

B is for baby Betty with a bonnet

P is for pudgy Patty with a ponytail

Without me to help guard the spider, Sam got all the way to the spider's head before the girls chased him away!

Without morning recess, it seemed like a veeeeery long time until lunch. I got hot lunch today, which I hardly ever do, because it was "chicken nuggets, carrot sticks, potato chips, fruit chews, and milk variety"—everything I like.

I'm not sure what the lunch ladies are named but they are both very smiley.

(This is supposed to be the lunch ladys hand, not some random, floating hand)

One of them has really big hands and gave me an extra big helping of chips. The other one has a little accent.

Dis izza goot lunch, dis one

My neighbor (who is pretty old herself) said that they were the lunch ladies when SHE was in school.

After lunch, everyone gave little speeches about why they wanted to be President.

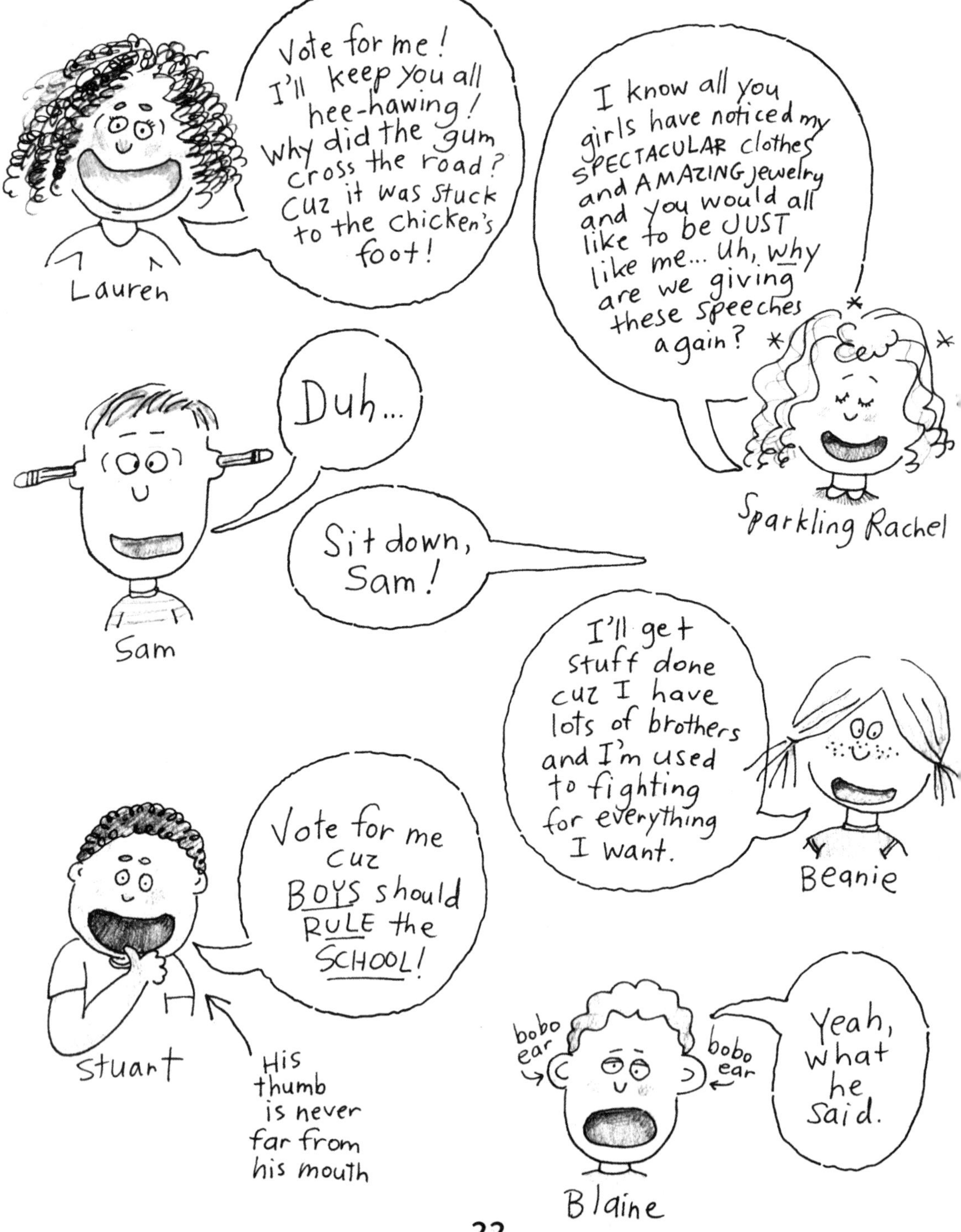
Vote for me! I'll keep you all hee-hawing! Why did the gum cross the road? Cuz it was stuck to the chicken's foot!
Lauren
I know all you girls have noticed my SPECTACULAR clothes and AMAZING jewelry and you would all like to be JUST like me... Uh, why are we giving these speeches again?
Sparkling Rachel
Duh...
Sit down, Sam!
Sam
I'll get stuff done cuz I have lots of brothers and I'm used to fighting for everything I want.
Beanie
Vote for me cuz BOYS should RULE the SCHOOL!
Stuart
His thumb is never far from his mouth
Yeah, what he said.
bobo ear
bobo ear
Blaine

Cammy: I talked my mother into letting me get an extra hole in my ear -- Has everyone noticed it by the way?-- which means I can do ANYTHING.

Kate: You HAVE to vote for me because my dopey brother was VICE president of HIS class and just ONCE I'd like to beat him at something!

Annie: I think I would make a good prethident becuth I am a thmart perthun and I work hard.

Griffin: I'm good at bossing people around and that's what the President does

Titus: Vote for me because I'm wonderful... BLAH BLAH BLAH ...Wisconsin is so great... BLAH BLAH BLAH ...and I look like someone's father... BLAH BLAH BLAH

(I made that up because I don't remember what he said, but you can bet it was something dopey like that.)

Dillon Cobb: Mrs. T? The flibosity of these speeches is foneticaly spatorious.

23

I said that I would try to make the school a better place for fourth graders. Meredith clapped very loudly. After that, everyone secretly wrote down the name of the person they want to be President. Mrs. T will tell us on Monday which two kids got the most votes. . . .

I have my fingers crossed!

wow!
This →
hand
came
out
so good!

September 22

I can't wait to find out who won the primary election on Friday! I HOPE I won!! Mrs. T said we would find out after PE and Music. It will feel like a very long time because PE is line dancing and Music is playing recorders. Our class stinks at both of those.

11:50 a.m.

JUST CALL ME CANDIDATE DILLY!!

Of course everyone voted for themselves except that Meredith voted for me and Dillon voted for Titus Stout, the new boy. So now it will be me against Titus, which means I'll win 'cause there are more girls in the class than boys and NO girl would EVER vote for a boy—YEA!!!! **THE PRESIDENCY IS MINE!!!!**

I told Lauren that when I am President, she will be my court jester. She will be in charge of making me laugh heartily at least 3 times a day.

What was the President's name in 1970? WHAT? You don't know? The same as it is now!

I wonder if I should change my name. Lots of real Presidents did. Gerald Ford was born Leslie King. I guess he changed it because it's a girly name. Or maybe I could get a fun nickname. Dilly is a nickname, but it's not as much fun as Grover Cleveland's nickname: "Uncle Jumbo." Now THAT'S a good one.

I am sitting next to Sam this week. He picks at his ear with his pencil eraser. Ew.

September 24

I made sure I wore red, white, and blue today so that I looked presidential. Meredith wore red, white, and blue, too, because she's my campaign manager.

Last night Mer and I talked on the phone about our campaign strategy. We made a list of the things we figured kids would want in a President—you know, someone who's fair, nice, smart, blah, blah, blah. Then she stayed up really late and made me posters that say stuff like:

We hung them up in the classroom and the hallway. We even put one on the back of a stall door in the girls' bathroom so that anyone sitting in there will have something to read. I feel famous!

Titus hasn't put up any posters yet. He did bring in a bag of Skittles today and he gave some to every kid in the class—even me.

HEY! I think I'll vote for TITUS instead of MYSELF because he gave me CANDY!

Yeah, right!

Poor Beanie. She was bummed out because she always has to wear her brothers' hand-me-downs. Today she was wearing boys jeans with no flare at all! She even has to wear her brothers' sneakers!
I told her not to worry because when President Carter was a boy, he had to wear ladies shoes to school on account of his father ordered too many pairs for his store so his family had to wear them so they wouldn't be wasted.

September 26

Lauren's latest joke:

hey Dilly!! Did you hear about the kidnapping in New York? well... They woke him up! HA HA HA!! ♡ Lauren

Blaine stars in "DUMBOY"

September 29

I am so glad today is Monday (even if I DO have to sit next to Blaine and his bobo ears this week).

Usually I am not a big Monday fan, but my little brother Matthew is pretending that he is a dog these days and he followed me around the whole weekend trying to lick me. It was pretty gross.

Today Titus and I made our speeches in front of the class about why we would be good as Class President. I went first. I said the stuff that Meredith and I had talked about before we made the posters, like I would be fair and nice to everyone and try to get lots of good things done for the class.

Then Titus talked about all this great stuff he had done at his old school. Hey, who's gonna call Wisconsin and check up on him? Maybe he just made it up to get votes. Well, he can make up all the stuff he wants because there's no way any of the girls in our class would ever vote for a boy, so he's gonna lose.

The other kids got to ask us questions.

Titus shook my hand after the speeches like we were 40 years old or something. I can't figure him out. He acts like he wants to win but so far he's just tried to get votes with candy. He still hasn't put up any posters. . . . And he doesn't seem to understand that the boys are outnumbered. I don't trust him for some reason. . . .

September 30

I never liked Griffin very much and now I have a good reason! He started the Titus for President Club today!

And they kicked the girls out of the SPIDER so they can meet in there and figure out how to make Titus win!

The teacher on duty didn't even _care!_

At recess Griffin handed out little cards to all the boys in 4T.

★ OFFICIAL MEMBER ★
TITUS FOR PRESIDENT
CLUB
Titus needs EVERY vote in the class! He will be the BEST class president!

The boys had a very long and very quiet meeting in the spider. Then I saw Griffin teaching everyone a secret club handshake. . . . And then I saw Beanie and Cammy trying to copy the handshake later! TRAITORS!

I was so MAD! I guess I said something about Titus' last name. I was <u>NOT</u> being mean! I was just explaining that "stout" means "fatso." I was just telling the TRUTH. Then <u>everybody</u> ganged up on me!

I never thought Dilly was so manifubusly mean!

Poor Titus... He can't help it if his name is weird

Ooooh, yes.... Poooooor Titus.......

30

OK. So that backfired.
I have to lay low. I just have
this really bad feeling all of a
sudden...

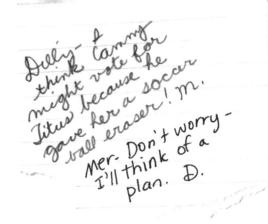

Dilly-
Cammy & I
think Titus
might vote for he
because he
gave her a soccer
ball eraser! m.

mer- Don't worry-
I'll think of a
plan. D.

October 2

We missed D.E.A.R. (Drop Everything And Read) time
today because a very tall man with shiny black hair came
and gave us all "Smoke-Choke-Croak" pencils if we
promised never to smoke cigarettes. Titus and Griffin
took pencils even though I bet they WILL smoke
someday because they are so DUMB (and then they'll
have to give
back their pencils).   SMOKE, CHOKE, CROAK

Dumb old Titus brought lollipops for everyone in the
Titus Club. I THINK I saw Cammy hide one in her
backpack but I'm not sure. How could a GIRL even THINK
of voting for a dopey BOY? HOW HOW HOW????

I'm losing ground fast. I guess my posters about being
nice and fair aren't enough. I told Meredith we should
start a Dilly for President Club or start giving out candy
and erasers like Titus but she said that the other kids
would think we were copycats. This is a tough one.

31

Poor Lauren. Yesterday was a bad day for her, too. She put her fish in the toilet while she was cleaning the fish bowl and by mistake she flushed Monday.

I said at least it wasn't Friday because Friday is everyone's favorite. I made her a sympathy card.

Hope she votes for me.

October 5

I KNEW Titus couldn't be trusted! Griffin and some other goofy boys from the Titus Club put up HIS posters today—just 5 days before the election:

TITUS doesn't pick HIS nose!
Take away P.E.? TITUS won't stand for it!
He NEVER tattles on other kids!
TITUS doesn't want seating assignments!
TITUS doesn't take gyps in line!
TITUS won't get rid of holiday parties!
NO PIZZA on Fridays?
TITUS won't let THAT happen!
VOTE FOR TITUS

I said, "Hey, I wouldn't
do those things either!"
Mer said, "She sure wouldn't!"

Then later, Meredith found
a note on the floor:

←

Now Titus is trying to buy Lauren's vote with a BUNNY!

I wish Titus would go back to Wisconsin and take all
the cheese in Connecticut with him. I can not STAND him!

Meredith and I decided it's time to change our strategy.
We don't have much time. I think that's why Titus waited
so long to put up his mean posters. He knew it wouldn't
give me time to get him back! Grrrrr!

I told Meredith that I needed to tell the kids some really cool things that I would do when I was Class President, like maybe have a day when we could all dress up as our favorite person from history or walk to the park and have our lunch there on nice days—stuff like that.

But this sure won't be the easy win I was expecting.
DARN.

October 6

Ever since we found Lauren's note, everyone is passing notes in code now so if they get intercepted, only your friends can read them.

Meredith and I spent our entire D.E.A.R. time trying to figure out one that we found crumpled up next to the computer. We finally got it. It says, "Thanks for the alien key chain, Titus. You have MY vote!"

It's signed
Annie!

October 7, Three Days to the Election

I've been really working the recess crowd for votes. It's a lot harder than I thought it would be. Sometimes I hear myself say things I wasn't even planning to say.

Me: "I think that on nice days we should be able to eat lunch outside! And maybe on the Friday right before a vacation, we should be able to vote on a video we could watch.... Wouldn't that be fun?"

Cammy: "Those are okay ideas, but what are you going to do about math homework? I hate math homework!"

me, working so hard for votes that I'm sweating

← some weird first grader being nosy

TITUS RULES

Kate: "Me too! I HATE math homework!"

Me: "Well, maybe we could ask for no math homework on certain weeks..."

Cammy: "I'll bet Titus could get us NO math homework at ALL!"

Me: "Well, well ... okay ... when I'M President, no more math homework. In fact, no more homework at all!"

All the kids: "Hear, hear!!!"

Beanie: "And I don't like getting up early to catch the bus."

Me: "The bus driver should wait until you call him to say you're ready to go!"

All the kids: **"YEA!"**

Rachel: "I don't like sitting next to Dillon Cobb. He snorts when he reads to himself."

Me: "No girl should EVER have to sit next to a boy!"

Lauren: "Scary Mrs. Barry scares me!"

Me: "Barry's out! GONE! No scary grown-ups at schoc when I'm in charge!"

After recess, Meredith started passing me notes like CRAZY.

> Dilly! That's not what we talked about! You can't promise stuff like that! m.
>
> Mer - You worry too much. —Dilly
>
> D - But how are you going to do all of those things? m
>
> Mer, I'll figure that out after the election. Right now I'm just trying to WIN! D.
>
> Big mistake Dilly.

I definitely won some votes today. Dilly's BACK IN THE RACE! And soon Dilly will RETAKE THE LEAD!!!

October 8, Two Days to the Election

Meredith and I got together after school yesterday pretending to do spelling homework but really I was telling her all about my new poster ideas. She didn't seem all that excited, but I told her it was the only way to win. I think she's being an old worrywart.

I made the posters after dinner and put them up FIRST THING today. (I missed morning recess to do it. And I also never actually did my spelling homework, but this election is MUCH more important than HOMEWORK.)

Here's what my NEW posters say:

I campaigned hard at recess again.

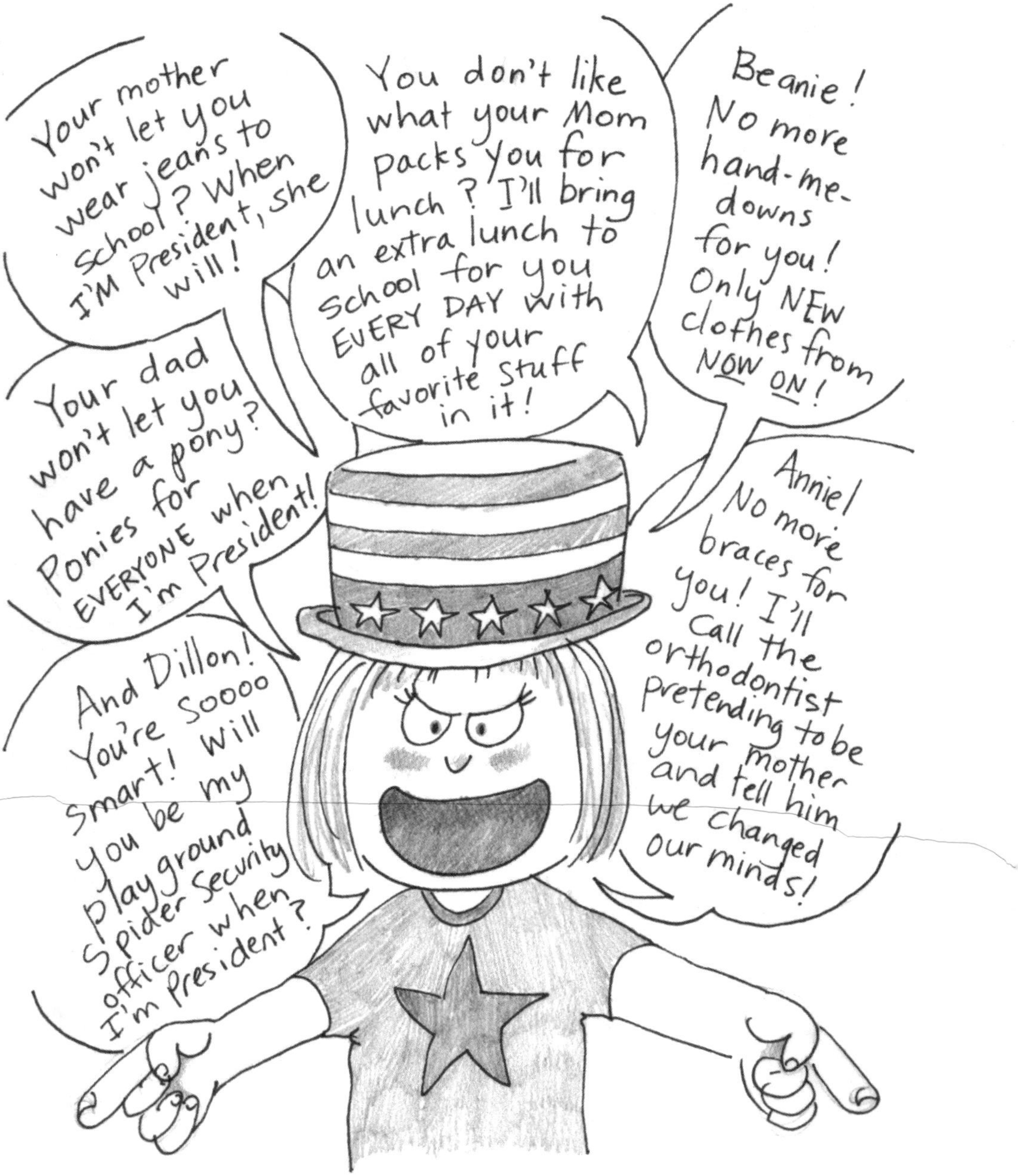

Vote Count:

Titus	Me	Not Sure
Griffin	Meredith	Dillon Cobb
Sam	Beanie	Cammy
Blaine	Lauren	Annie
Stuart	Kate	Rachel

It's anybody's presidency now.

October 9, ONE DAY LEFT

Mr. Cunningham told
Mr. Williams, the custodian,
to take down my posters.
Mrs. T said he didn't like
the stuff about no homework
and shorter school days.
I think he's worried that
after I become President,
I'll run for PRINCIPAL.

Poor Lauren. Her fish are dropping like flies. Only
Tuesday, Friday, and Chuck are left. (I told her I'd buy her
more fish if I become President.)

Because tomorrow's the election, Mrs. T was talking
about the importance of being a good winner and a
good loser.

Yeah, right.

Like President Jimmy Carter said, "Show me a good
loser and I'll show you a loser."

No time to write more . . . I gotta get more votes.
I think I can win Dillon Cobb over if I promise him double
lunches every day. And Rachel might give me her vote
if I promise her a fourth grade fashion show twice a
year featuring her.

TOMORROW IS THE
BIG DAY!!
(I don't really
have a toe ring
but I would
like one)

October 10, ELECTION DAY!

I WON!!! It's over! I did it!

(Mrs. T said I won by 1 vote! Thank goodness I voted for myself!)

I am the PRESIDENT! HAIL TO THE CHIEF-ESS!

The first thing I'm going to do (after I arrange for a couple of random detentions for Titus and Griffin) is get a pet raccoon like President Calvin Coolidge had.

And I also think I need a middle initial.

Dilly B. Duncan.

Dilly E. Duncan.

Oh no. That's **DED.**

I don't have to worry about what the initial stands for. President Harry S. Truman had a middle initial that didn't stand for anything. The **S.** just stood for **S.**

Today:
Fuller School

Tomonrow:
The White House!

But now, TIME TO CELEBRATE MY AMAZING VICTORY!!! TITUS LOST AND I WON! HA!

October 13

I tried to get together with Meredith over the weekend so we could think up some laws we can pass to punish Griffin and Titus and anybody who didn't vote for me. I left a couple of messages on her machine but I guess she was really busy because she never called me back.

That was OK, though, because I played with Matt. He stopped being a dog so we could finally play a FUN game. We played "Dilly is President and Matt is the adoring public." He just had to do whatever I told him and bow to me a lot.

First thing today, at morning recess, a bunch of kids congratulated me on my victory. They said they liked all of the ideas I had when I was running. Kate even asked for my autograph.

(The adoring public)

Everyone gave me gyps in line because I am, after all, the President. I tried to take Meredith with me but she said she didn't want to be rude. Silly her.

Right after D.E.A.R. time, Mrs. T split the class into the Senate and the House of Representatives. (Congress will be in session in two days, although as I am the President, I can probably change that if I want to.) Mer is in the House (Beanie's the head of it) and Mrs. T made dopey Titus the head of the Senate.

Now my name is on the blackboard (which is, interestingly, green) under Mrs. T's name. It says, "Class President: Dilly Duncan." I am beginning to feel quite famous.

October 14

I've been thinking. My desk should be in front of the class, next to Mrs. T's, not in a row with all of the regular kids. And I should have some sort of badge or medal, so that kids in other classes realize that I am the President!

After snack time, I made a whole list of things I should be able to do now that I'm President. It took me so long that I never got around to my Math worksheet. But I just added it to my list: The President should have someone who does her Math FOR her.

When we got outside for recess, a bunch of mean kids started bugging me.

45

October 15

I told Mrs. T that I needed to stay in for recess this afternoon and look up some information on presidential things in the library. Really I just wanted to keep away from all those annoying kids who follow me around the playground asking when they're getting their ponies and when Mr. Cunningham is going to announce that school will start later.

I don't even remember saying that stuff. Well, I don't remember saying ALL of it. I just need to avoid those kids until they forget about it. I'm kind of hoping that something will happen to distract them, like a huge hurricane or maybe someone famous like Britney Spears visiting our school. And I hope it happens SOON.

For now, they just bug Meredith if I'm not around. I don't think she minds because that's part of what you do as a best friend.

October 16

When we lined up to go into school this morning, I took my place at the front of the line like I have all week. It is my presidential spot. But THIS time, Griffin got all mad and told me to move because he said it wasn't fair that I got to be first every day. I told him the President ALWAYS goes first but he wouldn't listen. I think he's still mad because I beat Titus. My mom calls stuff like that "sour grapes."

No one really talked to me very much all morning, even in P.E. Cammy asked Meredith to be her partner for sit ups so I had to be partners with Dillon Cobb.

Then at lunch, I was the last one there because I needed to use the bathroom. No one saved me a seat so I had to sit at a table by myself. Well, not exactly ALL by myself. At the other end of the table were a couple of weird second grade boys who spent the whole lunch period blowing into their milk. Meredith didn't even move over to sit with me.

There are 2 possible reasons that no one wanted to sit with me:

Possible Reason #1

I brought hard-boiled eggs and even through the bag they smelled pretty bad. (Of course President Richard Nixon's favorite lunch was cottage cheese and ketchup and HIS friends still ate with HIM.)

Dilly

Possible Reason #2

When we lined up to go to lunch, I told everyone they had to follow proper etiquette when dining with the President: when the President enters the room, everyone must stand. The President is always served her meal first. No one is allowed to leave the table before the President does. (I just read that last night in a book about presidents I borrowed from the library.)

I'm hoping it was the eggs. I get the best lunches the day after Mom goes to the grocery store and the worst ones the day before she goes. I think she needs to make a trip.

Mom did pack me a sticker in my lunch that said "Best Friends" but since I have no one to give it to right now I will stick it on the back of this journal.

It IS lonely at the top.

At least tomorrow, I will get to do presidential things. That's what Mrs. T said.

October 17

Today was the day I got to do official stuff as President but CHECK THIS OUT! All I did was sit by myself in the hall waiting for the Congress to send me laws and then I just vetoed them or signed them! I didn't get to make any laws at all!

And the only thing one of the Senators (Blaine) brought me was some dopey law about having a "Bubble Gum Day." I'M supposed to get BRACES soon and then I won't be able to chew gum so. . . . VETO!

I asked Mrs. T whether or not I could make laws myself and she said I would have to talk about my ideas with the members of Congress! Gee, let's think this one out. . .

Titus is the head of the Senate and Beanie, who told me today that she is mad at me for not getting her new clothes like I promised, is the head of the House of Representatives! Yeah, like THEY are really going to help get MY laws passed.

I begged Mrs. T to let me have indoor recess again because the other kids are driving me nuts, but she said no.

So I go outside and all I hear is:

"Hey Dilly! How come I still have a nasty bus driver?"

"Yeah! Where's our two-hour snack?"

Then, Griffin says, "She's not keeping any of her promises, is she?"

Give me a break! I've only been President for a week! Jeepers!

The boys met in the spider just before recess ended. This time, Rachel, Beanie, Cammy, and Annie were with them. I thought I heard them talking about throwing me out of office. I hope I'm wrong. I hope they were talking about throwing me a party or something.

October 20

I tried talking to Beanie today about some of the promises I made when I was campaigning for the presidency but she wouldn't listen.

Mean Beanie: "Why did you veto our Bubble Gum Day?"

Poor Me: "Because it was dumb."

Mean Beanie: "Well that's what I think of YOUR ideas!"

Poor Me: "Well I'll go talk to Titus then!"

Mean Beanie: "Yeah, you do that. I bet he really likes you a lot ever since you beat him in the election."

Poor Me: "Well . . . well . . ."

October 21

School seems very long these days. Lunchtime is reeeeeaaaally long. I actually look forward to going home and playing Matt's owner (he's back to being a dog). This past weekend we played fetch a lot. It was fun . . . sort of.

I decided to stay after school to talk to Mrs. T. I told her the kids were mad at me for not keeping my promises. She just keeps saying that I should talk to members of Congress about passing some of the ideas I talked about during my campaign. I didn't tell her I already talked to Beanie and I don't even want to THINK about talking to Titus.

I am going to have to walk home from school now because I missed the bus.

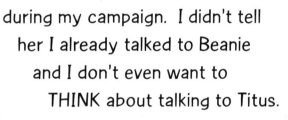

Why is Dilly still awake??

Poooor Dilly

Poooor Dilly

(those weird bugs that come out at night)

I can't sleep anymore because of my presidential responsibilities

53

October 22

Nobody in my class likes me anymore. Today at recess I played with a bunch of second graders. I could always drop out of school. President Andrew Johnson did and he didn't even learn to read or write until he was a TEENAGER.

Even Meredith has turned against me. She keeps asking when we're getting our special fourth grade extra vacation. I'm like, "MEREDITH! Don't you remember that we just said all that stuff to get me elected??!"

I'd like to go back to just being a regular citizen. I had lots more friends back then.

October 23

I got a bunch of stuff from Congress today. Since everyone is being VERY MEAN to me, I am going to use my . . .

VETO POWER!

Proposed law: Recycle milk cartons at lunch.	→	**President Dilly's response:** VETO! Too much work just to save some trees.
Proposed law: Black and Red Day to honor school colors.	→	**President Dilly's response:** VETO! I don't look good in black and red.
Proposed law: Offer chocolate milk at snack in addition to regular milk.	→	**President Dilly's response:** VETO! I bring tangerine juice from home so I don't care about having dumb old chocolate milk at snack.

I could hear the kids yelling in the classroom when Titus went back into the Senate and told them about all of my vetos—HA HA Titus.

I am really looking forward to dismissal today.

ORDER! ORDER IN THE SENATE!!

I'll have a burger, fries, and a chocolate shake... No, make it strawberry!

(Lauren's still the funniest kid in the whole country, even if she does hate me.)

October 24

Ms. Fee, the school counselor, came in to talk to our class today. She always dresses like a kid. I think she does that 'cause she thinks she'll fool some dopey kid into thinking she IS a kid and then he'll tell her all his problems. Last year, Lauren told me she has a tattoo!

Usually she visits the classes when there are problems. I bet Mrs. T told her we are having political trouble.

As soon as she walked in today, everyone raised their hands to go to the bathroom like they always do. But I think she's wised up to that one 'cause she wouldn't let anyone go (and I actually think Dillon Cobb really HAD to go, so I kind of felt sorry for him).

Mrs. Fee stood in front of the class and said, "Today we're going to talk about 'I CARE' language. I feel BLANK when you BLANK. Example: I feel SAD when you are MEAN. Does anyone else have an example?"

Blah blah blah. I actually think I did fall asleep during the last part because I remember her talking about the meaning of "compromise" and then the next thing I remember is seeing her wrap up a puppet show between two monkeys who were having trouble COMPROMISING. I think I missed a solid 20 minutes in there.

She did give us cool key chain thingamajiggers before she left. I asked Mrs. T if I could be excused to go out into the hall and attach it to my backpack and she said that she would do it for me while we were silently reading a chapter in our Science books.

Right now Meredith is holding up a painting she did in Art and bragging about how she made it. I'm writing this so I don't have to listen. I know we're going to get dismissed late and I'm going to have to RUN to catch the bus.

Blah blah blah I'm so great Blah blah blah

October 27

GUESS WHAT?!

I ended up with TITUS'S backpack on Friday!

Mrs. T put my key chain on HIS backpack and I grabbed it because I was in a rush!

I opened it when I got home, thinking it was mine, and I found Titus's sweatshirt and lunchbox in there. I also found his journal. I know I wasn't supposed to look in it, but I did anyway. It felt pretty weird to be reading someone else's private stuff. I copied down some of what he wrote:

"It is really hard being the new kid and not knowing anybody. The boys in the class are OK. The girls seem pretty nice, too. There is a girl named Cammy who is pretty. So is a girl named Dilly. I miss my friends back in Wisconsin a lot, especially Leah because we have known each other since kindergarten."

"I think I will run for Class President. I probably won't win but at least more kids will get to know me."

"My mom knows that I don't really have any friends yet so she is trying to help me. She gave me Skittles to share with everyone and a bunch of stuff like mini erasers. I don't think kids will like you just because you give them stuff, but I guess it can't hurt."

"Today was such a great day! A bunch of boys made up the Titus for President Club! I think they really like me! Griffin even offered to make posters. (I actually had made some Vote for Titus posters myself but I didn't want to hurt Griffin's feelings so I'll use his when he makes them.)"

"I think my speech today was pretty good. I talked about some things we did at my old school that would be pretty fun to do here, too."

"Griffin put up some posters for me today. I don't really like them because they seem kind of mean, but I don't want to hurt his feelings. I'm not really sure what I should do."

"Tomorrow is the election! I think I have a pretty good chance of winning! I know the kids in the Club are counting on me."

"Today was the worst day ever. I lost the election. I hope the kids will still be friends with me. At least I am the head of the Senate. I can probably get some good things done for the other kids as the head of the Senate."

"I think Dilly hates me. I don't know why! I mean, she beat me in the election and I don't hate her! But she keeps writing VETO on all the things we have worked on in the Senate! I know I should ask her why, but she's not as nice as she was when school first started."

I read Titus's whole journal. I felt really bad about doing it. I know it was wrong. But I also know there is something I can do to kind of make up for it.

October 28

I asked Titus to stay after school with me yesterday so that we could work out some compromises (just like those dopey puppets of Mrs. Fee's). He said, "Sure." I wrote down all the promises that I could remember making while I was running for President. Then we thought about ways we could keep as many of them as possible.

Today we stood up in front of the class and announced some new laws that we would propose to Congress. They have to be voted on in the House of Representatives AND the Senate, so they might not all make it, but we'll see.

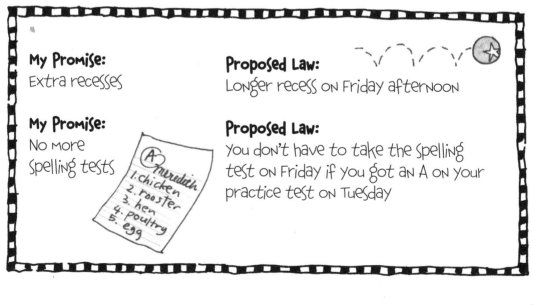

My Promise:
Extra recesses

Proposed Law:
Longer recess on Friday afternoon

My Promise:
No more Spelling tests

Proposed Law:
You don't have to take the Spelling test on Friday if you got an A on your practice test on Tuesday

Meredith
1. chicken
2. rooster
3. hen
4. poultry
5. egg

My Promise:
NO HOMEWORK

My Promise:
Class parties every week

My Promise:
Girls will never have
to sit next to boys

My Promise:
Ponies for everyone

My Promise:
No more scary
grown-ups
at school

Proposed Law:
ONE NO HOMEWORK coupon for each kid
to be used anytime during the year

Proposed Law:
Add a class party on May Day

Proposed Law:
No assigned seats for the
last two weeks of school

Proposed Law:
Bring your pet to school Day

Proposed Law:
Couldn't do much with this one.
Let's hope everyone forgot.

I don't think the Supreme Court will have any problems
with our laws because she was smiling a lot after Titus
and I spoke to the class.

And then Meredith saved me a place at lunch, even
though I had hard-boiled eggs.

October 30

Everybody was all happy today cuz it was Hat and Movie Day (the House and Senate passed that law yesterday). We watched "Old Yeller" and got to wear hats INSIDE the building.

Blaine even THANKED me. (Of course then he had to remind me that he still has a nasty bus driver. I told him I'd talk to Titus and Beanie about it and see what we can do.)

Tomorrow is Halloween!

Meredith is wearing her chicken costume again.

Every year she wears her chicken costume and every year someone thinks she's Big Bird and she gets SOOOO mad!

Guess who? ↪

I am dressing up as Abraham Lincoln. Titus is dressing up as his wife, Mary Todd Lincoln. We decided to keep it a secret until the school's Halloween parade after lunch. It is going to be SO funny!

Here's what I'm going to look like in my Lincoln costume. Won't I look just like him?

I'm glad I'm not the REAL President. Being President is not what I expected. I don't think I want to go into politics after all this. I might want to be a hairdresser. Or a shepherd.

"Dilly had a little lamb..."

(These are supposed to be sheep even though they look like poodles)

(By the way, President Woodrow Wilson kept a flock of sheep on the White House lawn to keep the grass short!)

But for now, like President Reagan said, "Together, we're going to do what has to be done."

A+ Super Journal!
(And I'll try to get that
squeak out of my desk
drawer so that it's not as
obvious when I'm sneaking
a Tootsie Roll!)

♡ Mrs. T